WHAT WHAT WHAT?

ARATA TENDO • RYOJI ARAI

TRANSLATED FROM
THE JAPANESE BY
DAVID BOYD

ENCHANTED LION BOOKS
NEW YORK

What's he like?

In a word, annoying. To a lot of people, anyway. In a room of ten kids,
he's almost always the odd one out.

Before he was born, his parents thought he'd be the next Mozart.
But music just isn't his thing.

He likes soccer, almost as much as being "it" in hide-and-seek,
but he can't keep the ball in the air for more than three kicks.

He really likes the Hubble telescope and the triceratops, so he reads
lots of books about outer space and dinosaurs. Just not when they have
too many words! Books like that put him to sleep.

But that doesn't mean he doesn't like learning stuff. Not even close!
He loves to learn and always wants to know everything about everything.

どーした

What's his name?
Pan, which means "everything."
Wherever he goes, his questions go, too.

His life goes something like this:
Pan hears his mom scream in the kitchen.
He runs in and asks, "What's wrong, Mom? What is it?"
"I saw a roach," she says.
"You saw a roach? Then what? What happened next?"
"To the roach? It ran away."
"What about you? Are you okay, Mom?"
"I'm fine now," she says. "Thanks, Pan."

Totally normal, right? But with Pan, things don't end there.
"Hey, Mom," he says. "Mom? Where do you think that roach went?
What if there are more roaches in the house?"
What what what?
Pan asks questions until his mom finally loses it.
"Stop scaring me, Pan! I'm trying to cook dinner!"

Pan hears his dad groan at the TV on a Sunday afternoon.
He rushes in and asks, "What happened, Dad? What's wrong?"
His dad's favorite team just lost in the bottom of the ninth.
"They lost? What happens now?"
"What do you mean?"
"What happens to the team?"
"They go home."
"Then what?"
"They'll work even harder next time, just like your old man."

Maybe things should have stopped there, but not with Pan.
Instead, he asks, "Work? Oh, yeah, you said you're behind on work.
But haven't you been watching TV all day? Shouldn't you be working?"
Pan keeps going until his dad finally snaps, "Pan, it's Sunday!"

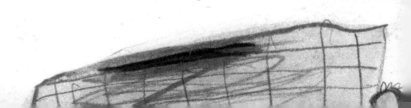

Pan sees his sister sitting on the couch, making an angry face like a tiger.
He asks, "What are you making that face for? What happened?"
"Listen to this," she says. Then she tells Pan all about school,
about her friends, about how Mom and Dad never listen to her.
Pan asks, "And then? And then? And then?"
She keeps going.
When she's done, she sighs and says, "I feel so much better now."
She ruffles her brother's hair and gets up from the couch.

Maybe Pan could have let things stop there. Except, well, he couldn't.
"Then what?" he asks. "What happens next?"
His sister yells, "The story's over, Pan! Weren't you listening?"
Then she storms off, even angrier than before.

Pan talks to everyone, even people he doesn't know.
In the park, he sees a little girl crying and goes over.
"Why are you crying?"
She points at a balloon way up in the sky.
"That balloon is yours? It got away?"
She nods.
"You're wondering how to get it back?"
She nods again. "Can you get it back for me?"

"Sorry! I don't know how to fly yet," says Pan.
The girl starts crying all over again.
That's when any other kid would walk away.
But not Pan.
"Why are you crying again?"
"Because my balloon hates me."
"What if it flew up there to keep a better eye on you?
Maybe it thinks you look even cuter from up there!"
The girl screams, "I'm not cute!" She sticks out her tongue at Pan.
Then she waves goodbye to her balloon and runs off to play.

I know, Pan thinks. *I'll call Grandma and Grandpa.*

They'll know what to do.

"Grandma, Grandpa, why does everyone always get mad at me?"

Pan's grandparents love it when he calls to ask questions.

Nobody else ever calls to ask them anything.

Pan asks, "What are you doing?"

"We were just watching TV."

"Why?"

"Because we didn't have anything else to do."

"Why didn't you go outside?"

"Because we were hoping you'd call."

"Really? Why?"

"Because we like talking to you."

"But why?"

"Pan, slow down a little. Maybe people get mad because you keep asking

questions. First, they're happy, but then it can get a little … annoying."

"So you mean I should stop asking questions?"

"No, but what if you ask one or two and then hold the rest in?"

No answer.

"Hello? Pan? Are you there?"

Nothing.

Then they hear him gasping for breath.

"How am I supposed to breathe if I keep everything in?"

When Pan sees a pretty woman crying on a park bench, he stops kicking his ball.

"What's the matter? Why are you crying?"

She doesn't say anything, but she looks so sad that Pan tries again.

"Are you okay?"

The woman sniffles, then says, "Please go away."

Any other kid would just go away.

But not Pan.

He sees a ripped-up photograph on the ground.

"What's that? Is it yours? Who's the man in the picture?"

"Just mind your own business."

The woman looks really angry now.

Then a cool guy walks over and asks her the very same question:

"What's the matter?"

This time, she looks sort of happy about it. "I don't know what to do," she says.

"Do you want to get some coffee and talk about it?"

"Okay," she says, getting up. They walk away.

Left alone with the pigeons, Pan asks, "What was that all about?"

There's a man on the bridge, watching the trains go by.

No one seems to notice him.

As the sun starts to set, the man climbs up the fence.

Pan sees him on his way home from soccer and calls out:

"Hey, what are you doing up there? It's dangerous! What if you fall?"

The man turns and says, "I, I won't…I just wanted to see the sunset."

"Why?"

"I thought it would be pretty."

"So now what?"

"What do you mean?"

"Are you coming down?"

"I was about to."

The man comes down.

"Shouldn't you go home?" Pan continues. "It's almost time for dinner, and you look really hungry. I need to get home, too. Hey…what's wrong?"

"What do you mean?" asks the man.

"You're crying. Did I make you cry? Everyone's always getting mad at me."

"No, I just got something in my eye," the man says and wipes away his tears.

He says goodbye to Pan and starts walking home.

When he turns around for a last look at Pan, he doesn't look hungry anymore.

He actually looks like he's just had the best meal of his life.

One morning,
Pan wakes up really hungry.
He remembers the stash of
week-old candy he's been hiding.
   Nom nom nom...Now it's all gone!

After a few minutes, Pan isn't feeling so great. He goes to the bathroom
and doesn't come out for a long time. When he's done, it's already time
for class! As Pan runs to school, something catches his eye—a lumpy pile in
a corner of the park.

Pan stops to get a better look. *Is that...a boy?*

   "Hello? What's going on? Are you okay?"
   The boy looks up at Pan, but he doesn't look okay.
   Pan keeps talking. "What's that on your face? It's all blue and red...
   Is that supposed to be Halloween makeup or something?"
   "I guess so," says the other boy.
   "But isn't it too early for that? Why don't you take it off?"
   Pan wets a cloth at the water fountain.
   The boy presses the cloth against his face, but the colors don't come off.
   "Why won't it come off?" Pan asks. "Who put that stuff on you, anyway?"
   "The man who lives with my mom."
   "Does he know it doesn't come off? Why would he do that to you?"
   "He does it all the time..."

The school bell rings.

"I gotta go." Pan stands up.

"You go to that school?" the boy asks.

"Yup, what about you?"

"Me too. I'm in third grade."

"So am I!" says Pan.

"My classroom is at the end of the hall," says the boy.

"I'm two rooms down from there. Why haven't I seen you before?"

"I miss a lot of school."

"Are you going now? Come on."

"I'm not going."

"What's your name? I'll tell your teacher you're not coming."

"My name's Kai," says the boy. "But my teacher won't be surprised."

Pan tells the teacher down the hall that he saw Kai alone in the park.

The teacher seems to freeze, like he doesn't know what to say.

Pan asks, "What's going on with Kai?"

The teacher says, "I don't know. I'll ask him when he comes back."

But Kai isn't there the next day, and he's not in the park, either.

So Pan goes to Kai's teacher and asks, "What's going on with Kai?"

"I called his house and his mom said he was sick," the teacher says.

"Are you going to visit him at home?" Pan asks.

"I don't think so. I have a lot of work to do."

"Okay, I'll go then. I'll ask my friend where he lives."

"Wait, hold on," the teacher says, wiping sweat from his forehead.

"I'll go, I'll go."

The next day, Pan asks the teacher what happened.

"I went to his house yesterday, but no one was home."

"What happens next?" asks Pan. "Are you going to go again today?"

"I can't. I really have a lot to do. The other teachers and I have discussed it,
and we've decided it's best to have the Children's Center ask about Kai.
They know what they're doing. Don't worry, he'll be back in no time."

But Kai isn't at school the next day. Or the next. Or the day after that.

Pan asks his mom and dad about the Children's Center again and again.

He says he wants to go there to ask about Kai.

Pan won't give up, so his mom agrees to take him.

When they get there, the Center is really busy and the phone never stops ringing.

The woman behind the desk looks like she's really tired.

Pan walks up and asks her, "What's going on with Kai?"

The woman says, "I'm sorry, I can't share that information with you."

"But my son is really worried," his mom says. "He just wants to know if his friend is okay."

The woman says she has to go to the back and ask about it.

When she comes back, she looks even more tired than before.

"I'm really sorry, I wish I could help, but we've got rules. Don't worry, though.
We'll do everything we can."

But what about Pan? What can he do?

He's full of questions, but has nowhere to put them.

So Pan asks a classmate where Kai lives and goes straight there.
It's a huge apartment building. Pan finds Kai's door and starts knocking.
"Kai? What's going on? Are you in there? Hello?"
A harsh voice inside says, "Shut up out there!"
A man in dirty clothes opens the door.
"Where's Kai?" Pan asks. "Is he okay?"
"Who's asking?"
"I'm his friend."
"Well, your friend's not here."
"Where'd he go?"
"Nowhere. Now go home."
The man comes out into the hallway and gives Pan a mean look.
Pan really wants to go home, but he's not going to give up.
"What did you do to Kai? If you were a kid, if you were Kai,
what would you do?"

Just then, a neighbor comes out of her apartment.
When the man in dirty clothes sees her,
he locks his door and slinks off down the hall.
With the man out of sight, the neighbor quietly tells Pan,
"Kai's mom is out working all the time, even late at night.
Sometimes people come by, but the man tells them to go away."
"What's happening to Kai?" Pan asks.
"I don't know," says the neighbor. "It's none of my business."
Then she goes back into her apartment.

Pan starts knocking on Kai's door again.

"Kai? Are you in there? Can you hear me?"

He puts his ear to the door and hears something.

"Kai, it's me. The kid from the park. Are you there?"

A few seconds later, a weak voice comes through the door.

"Is he still out there?"

"No, it's just me. What's going on? Are you okay?"

"I'm hungry. I haven't eaten in a long time."

"Hold on," Pan says, "I'll be right back."

Pan runs home as fast as he can.

His mom isn't there, but his sister is home from school.

Pan tells her what's going on and asks her for some bread.

Now Pan's sister is worried, too, so she runs after him.
Her friends see her running and ask, "What's going on?"
She tells them, and they start running, too.

Then the friends of her friends see everyone running and ask, "What's going on?"
Other friends, their brothers and sisters—they all see the crowd and ask,
"What's going on?"

Everyone wants to know. The mailman, the grocer, the hairdresser,
the old couple from down the street, Snowball and Tabby...

It looks like the whole town is running behind Pan now.
And everyone wants to know the same thing: "What's going on?"

When they reach Kai's apartment, Pan puts his face against the door and asks,
"Are you there, Kai? I have food. Can you open the door?"
No answer. A voice in the crowd says, "Maybe no one's home."
But Pan isn't ready to give up. "Kai! Can you hear me? Are you there?"
He hears something hit the other side of the door.
Pan's sister says, "Did you hear that? He's in there!"
A policeman comes to the front of the crowd. "What's this all about?"

The policeman asks the super to open Kai's door.
As soon as it's unlocked, Kai falls into Pan's arms.
Pan says, "Kai? Can you hear me? Can you hear me?"

That night, Pan has a dream. There are fairies all around him,
tickling the back of his neck and under his arms.
"Fwahaha. Stop, please! Fwahahaha!"
The fairies ask, "What is it? What's wrong?"
Pan answers, "I'm ticklish! I can't take it! Fwahaha!"
But the fairies won't stop.

All the fairies have the faces of people Pan has met.
The girl who lost her balloon, the woman crying in the park,
the man watching trains from the bridge.
And in the very back, there's a fairy with Kai's face.
With a shy look, he reaches out to tickle Pan like the others.
"Fwahaha! Come on, please! Fwahahaha!"
Pan can't do anything but laugh and laugh.

Pan's mom tells him that Kai is doing a lot better.

Pan's dad tells him that the man in the dirty clothes is gone forever and Kai is safe.

Pan's sister tells him that it looks like he's going to get a medal for what he did.

But when Pan asks if he can go and play with Kai, no one knows what to tell him.

When Pan finally learns that Kai and his mom have moved far away, he cries all day.

He just wants to see his friend.

They never even had a chance to play together.

"Why? Why? Why did he have to go?"

Pan can't do anything but cry and cry.

Then a letter comes. It's from Kai.

On the front, it says,

To the boy who always asks questions.

Pan opens it. He reads the words out loud:

I want to say thank you. Thanks to you and all your questions,

my Halloween makeup finally came off.

I promise we'll play together some day, but I don't know when.

Even if we're bigger then and don't look the same, I'll still know it's you.

Because you'll look at me and ask,

"Are you okay? Where have you been? Is everything okay now?"

And I'll say back,

"Everything's fine with me. What's going on with you?"

Now, wherever Pan goes, that letter goes with him.
His mom says not to read it while he's walking,
but he does anyway.

One day on the way to school—BAM!
He walks right into a pole!
"Ow-ow! Hey, look at all the pretty stars…"

A girl comes over and asks,
"What happened? Did you hit your head? Are you okay?"
Suddenly, Pan's pain is gone. Just like that!
Pan asks the girl, "Huh? Why doesn't it hurt anymore?
Was that magic or something? What did you do?"

What what what what what what what what what…

Author's Note

"What's this book? Where did it come from?"

Oh, that's right. You've never heard the story of how you were born.

I'm not very good at drawing, but I always wanted to make my own picture book. So I thought it would be a lot of fun to write the story for one. I actually wrote some stories for children when I was younger. I even had Yoji Kuri, a very talented artist, do some artwork for me. But when I started writing stories for adults in my twenties, I guess I drifted away from that world.

Still, my love for picture books and children's stories was always there.

Then, one day, an editor named Kazuko Konno sent me an amazing picture book from Scandinavia. The story was pretty serious, but everyone loved it. Maybe that got me thinking. Not long after that, you came into my life.

Remember the first thing you asked me?

"Hey, what if you wrote about me?"

Only one way to find out, right? I wrote your story, then sent it to Konno-san to see what she thought. She loved it. We had only one question: Who should we ask to do the art? You know, there are a lot of talented artists out there, but we felt like you needed a very special artist—someone as bright and eager as you. Konno-san and I could think of only one artist who matched that description.

The first time I met him, I wore my elephant bus badge so that he would know what a huge fan of his work I am.

I'm talking about Ryoji Arai, of course. You know what he told me that very day? That he'd be happy to draw you. I couldn't believe my luck!

"So your strategy worked? He said yes because you had your badge on?"

I wonder. Anyway, I'm really glad I had the chance to work with him.

The same goes for Seiichi Suzuki, who came up with the beautiful design for the book. I also want to thank everyone at Shueisha who worked so hard to make this book a reality. And I want to thank everyone who got this book into bookstores, and everyone working in those bookstores. All of you have my deepest thanks!

Finally, I need to say something to you, Pan. I'm so glad we met. Thank you—for everything.

– Arata Tendo

Note to the reader

The Japanese title of *What What What?* is
Dōshita dōshita (pronounced "doe-sh-tah doe-sh-tah").

"*Dōshita*" is a versatile question, the meaning of which depends on its context:
What's up? What happened? What's the matter? So what? Why?

"*Dōshita*" is Pan's constant refrain.
The Japanese characters どーした appear in almost every spread of the book.

The climax of *What What What?* is an uproar of townspeople's voices,
the pages covered in Japanese characters. What do they say? You guessed it: "*Dōshita.*"

www.enchantedlion.com

First English-language edition copyright © 2017 by Enchanted Lion Books
67 West Street, 317A, Brooklyn, NY 11222
First published in Japan as *Doshita Doshita* by Shueisha Inc., Tokyo
Copyright © 2014 by Arata Tendo and Ryoji Arai
English translation rights arranged by Shueisha Inc. through Paper Crane Agency
English translation copyright © 2017 by David G. Boyd

ISBN 978-1-59270-237-4

Printed in China by R. R. Donnelley Asia Printing Solutions, Ltd.

First Printing

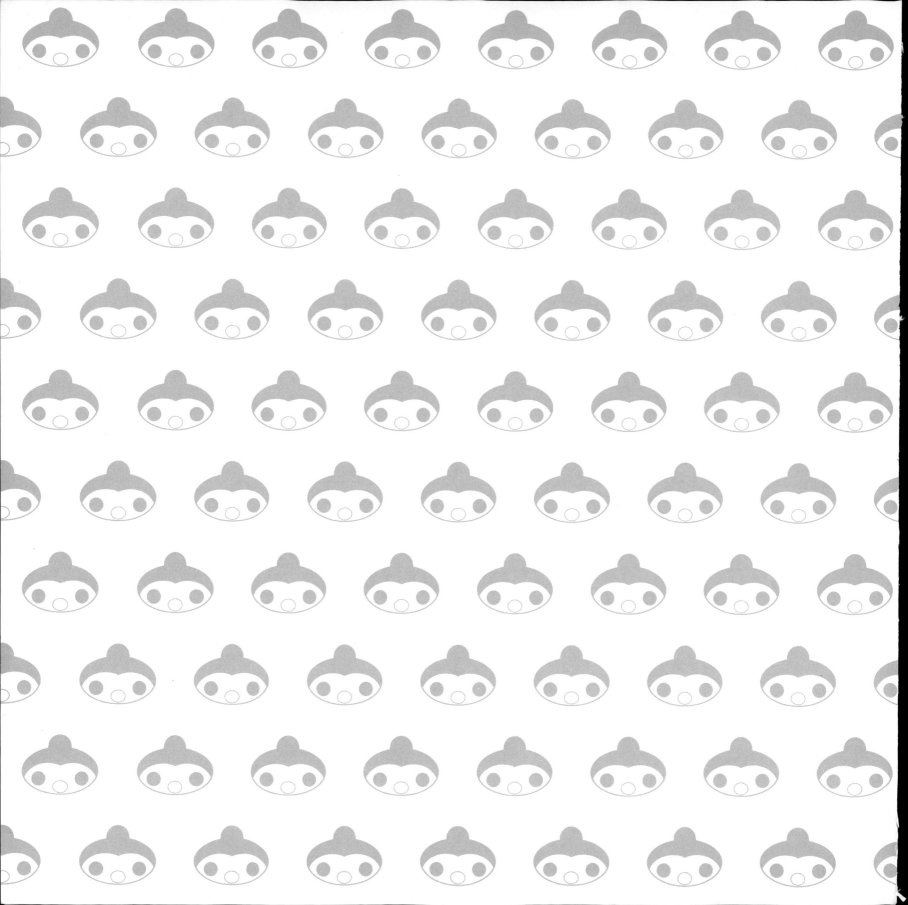